Japanese Children's
FAVORITE STORIES

Japanese Children's
FAVORITE STORIES

edited by

Florence Sakade

illustrated by

Yoshisuke Kurosaki

CHARLES E. TUTTLE COMPANY
Rutland, Vermont   *Tokyo, Japan*

Published by the Charles E. Tuttle Company, Inc.
of Rutland, Vermont & Tokyo, Japan
with editorial offices at Suido 1-chome, 2–6, Bunkyo-ku, Tokyo

© *1958 by Charles E. Tuttle Company, Inc.*

Library of Congress Catalog Card No. 58–11620
International Standard Book No. 0–8048–0284–x

First edition, 1953
Forty-second printing, 1993

PRINTED IN JAPAN

Stories in This Book

Publisher's Foreword

In the autumn of 1953 we published the first edition of this book, choosing the stories from the pages of *Silver Bells*, the English-language edition of one of Japan's leading children's magazines. Since then, although the magazine is no longer published, the book has been so popular that successive reprintings have worn the plates past further use, and still orders continue to pour in for it. To meet this continuing demand, we are pleased to offer the present revision, which contains ten of the best-loved stories from the first edition, ten new stories, and entirely new illustrations by one of Japan's foremost illustrators. We are confident the book will meet the same enthusiastic response—from children, parents, and teachers alike—as did the first edition, and should like to quote the following remarks from the Foreword to that edition:

Parents and teachers all over the world have become increasingly aware of the need to raise their children to be citizens of the world, to become thinking adults who, while proud of their own traditions and heritage, are free of the national prejudices, rivalries, and suspicions that have caused such havoc in the past. To this end they have wanted material that would give their children a sympathetic understanding of the life and culture of other lands. This book will fill some part of this need.

We have chosen those traditional stories that may in a very true sense be called " favorites." They have been loved by the children of Japan for hundreds of years, and have proven no less delightful to Western children, thus showing again that the stories that please the children of one land are likely to please children everywhere.

Each of these stories is to be found in Japan—and often in other countries too—in many forms and versions. We have tried to select the most interesting version in each case and, in our translations, to remain true to the spirit of the Japanese originals. At the same time we have inserted sufficient words of explanation into the text of the stories to make customs and situations that are peculiar to Japan intelligible to Western readers without the need for distracting notes.

Editorial responsibility for the book has been borne by Florence Sakade; both as a mother and as an editor and author of numerous children's publications she has had wide experience in the entertainment and education of children. The English versions are the work of Meredith Weatherby, well-known translator of Japanese literature.

Peach Boy

ONCE upon a time there was an old man and his old wife living in the country in Japan. The old man was a woodcutter. He and his wife were very sad and lonely because they had no children.

One day the old man went into the mountains to cut firewood, and the old woman went to the river to wash some clothes.

No sooner had the old woman begun her washing than she was very surprised to see a big peach come floating down the river. It was the biggest peach she'd ever seen in all her life. She pulled the peach out of the river and decided to take it home and give it to the old man for his supper that night.

Late in the afternoon the old man came home, and the old woman said to him: "Look what a wonderful peach I found for your supper." The old man said it was truly a beautiful peach. He was so hungry that he said: "Let's divide it and eat it right away."

So the old woman brought a big knife from the kitchen and was getting ready to cut the peach in half. But just then there was the sound of a human voice from inside the peach. "Wait! Don't cut me!" said the voice. Suddenly the peach split open, and a beautiful baby boy jumped out of the peach.

The old man and woman were astounded. But the baby said: "Don't be afraid. The God of Heaven saw how lonely you were without any children, so he sent me to be your son."

The old man and woman were very happy, and they took the baby to be their son. Since he was born from a peach, they named him Momotaro, which means Peach Boy. They loved Momotaro very much and raised him to be a fine boy.

When Momotaro was about fifteen years old, he went to his father and said: "Father, you have always been very kind to me. Now I am a big boy and I must do something to help my country. In a distant part of the sea there is an island named Ogre Island. Many wicked ogres live there, and they often come to our land and do bad things like carrying people away and stealing their things. So I'm going to go to Ogre Island and

fight them and bring back the treasure which they have there. Please let me do this."

The old man was surprised to hear this, but he was also very proud of Momotaro for wanting to help other people. So he and the old woman helped Momotaro get ready for his journey to Ogre Island. The old man gave him a sword and armor, and the old woman fixed him a good lunch of millet dumplings. Then Momotaro began his journey, promising his parents that he would come back soon.

Momotaro went walking toward the sea. It was a long way. As he went, along he met a spotted dog. The dog growled at Momotaro and was about to bite him, but then Momotaro gave him one of the dumplings. He told the spotted dog that he was going to fight the ogres on Ogre Island. So the dog said he'd go along too and help Momotaro.

Momotaro and the spotted dog kept on walking and soon they met a monkey. The spotted dog and the monkey started to have a fight. But

13

Momotaro explained to the monkey that he and the spotted dog were going to fight the ogres on Ogre Island. Then the monkey asked if he couldn't go with them. So Momotaro gave the monkey a dumpling and let the monkey come with them.

Momotaro and the spotted dog and the monkey kept on walking. Suddenly they met a pheasant. The spotted dog and the monkey and the pheasant were about to start fighting. But when the pheasant heard that Momotaro was going to fight the ogres on Ogre Island, he asked if he could go too. So Momotaro gave the pheasant a dumpling and told him to come along.

So, with Momotaro as their general, the spotted dog and the monkey and the pheasant, who usually hated each other, all became good friends and followed Momotaro faithfully. They walked a long, long way, and finally reached the sea. At the edge of the sea Momotaro built a boat. They all got in the boat and started across the sea toward Ogre Island.

When they came within sight of the island, they could see that the ogres had a very strong fort there. And there were many, many ogres. Some of them were red, some blue, and some black.

First the pheasant flew over the walls of the fort and began to peck at the ogres' heads. They all tried to hit the pheasant with their clubs, but he was very quick and dodged all their blows. And while the ogres weren't looking, the monkey slipped up and opened the gate of the fort. Then Momotaro and the spotted dog rushed into the fort and started fighting the ogres too.

It was a terrible battle! The pheasant pecked at the heads and eyes of the wicked ogres. And the monkey clawed at them. And the spotted dog bit them. And Momotaro cut them with his sword. At last the ogres were

completely defeated. They all bowed down low before Momotaro and promised never to do wicked things again. Then they brought Momotaro all the treasure they had stored in the fort.

It was the most wonderful treasure you can imagine. There was much gold and silver and many precious jewels. There was an invisible coat and hat, and a hammer that made a piece of gold every time you hit it on the ground, and many other wonderful things. Momotaro and his three helpers carried all this in their boat back to the land. Then they made a cart and put all the treasure in the cart and pulled it back to Momotaro's house.

How happy the old man and woman were when they saw their son return safely from Ogre Island! They were very rich now with all the treasure that Momotaro had brought, and they all lived together very, very, happily.

The Magic Teakettle

THERE was once a priest who was very fond of drinking tea. He always made the tea himself and was very fussy about the utensils he used. One day in an old secondhand shop he discovered a beautiful iron kettle used for boiling water when making tea. It was a very old and rusty kettle, but he could see its beauty beneath the rust. So he bought it and took it back to his temple. He polished the kettle until all the rust was gone, and then he called his three young pupils, who lived in the temple.

"Just look what a fine kettle I bought today," he said to them. "Now I'll boil some water in it and make us all some delicious tea."

So he put the kettle over a charcoal fire in a brazier, and they all sat around waiting for the water to boil. The kettle started getting hotter and hotter, and suddenly a very strange thing happened: the kettle grew the head of a badger, and a bushy badger tail, and four little badger feet.

"Ouch! it's hot!" cried the kettle. "I'm burning, I'm burning!" And with those words the kettle jumped off the fire and began running around the room on its little badger feet.

The old priest was very surprised, but he didn't want to lose his kettle. "Quick! quick!" he said to his pupils, "don't let it get away. Catch it!"

One boy grabbed up a broom; another, a pair of fire tongs; and the third, a dipper. And away the three of them went, chasing after the kettle. When they finally caught it, the badger head and the bushy badger tail and

the four little badger feet disappeared and it was just an ordinary kettle again.

"This is most strange," said the priest. "It must be a bewitched teakettle. Now, we don't want anything like that around the temple. We must get rid of it."

Just then a junkman came by the temple. So the priest took the kettle out to him and said: "Here's an old iron kettle I'll sell you very cheap, Mr. Junkman. Just give me whatever you think it's worth."

The junkman weighed the kettle on his hand scales and then he bought it from the priest for a very small price. He went home whistling, pleased at having found such a bargain.

That night the junkman went to sleep and all the house was very quiet. Suddenly a voice called: "Mr. Junkman. Oh, Mr. Junkman!"

The junkman opened his eyes. "Who's that calling me?" he said, lighting a candle.

And there he saw the kettle, standing by his pillow, with the badger head, and the bushy badger tail, and the four little badger feet. The junkman was very surprised and said, "Aren't you the kettle I bought from the priest today?"

"Yes, that's me," said the kettle. "But I'm not an ordinary kettle. I'm really a badger in disguise and my name is Bumbuku, which means Good Luck. That mean old priest put me over a fire and burned me, so I ran away from him. But if you'll treat me kindly and feed me well and never put me over a fire, I'll stay with you and help you make your fortune."

"Why, this is very strange," said the junkman. "How can you help me make my fortune?"

"I can do all sorts of wonderful tricks," said the kettle, waving his bushy badger tail. "So all you have to do is put me in a show and sell tickets to the people who want to see me do my tricks."

The junkman thought this was a splendid idea. The very next day he built a little theater out in his yard, and put up a big sign which said: "Bumbuku, The Magic Teakettle of Good Luck, and His Extraordinary Tricks."

Every day more and more people came to see Bumbuku. The junkman would sell tickets out front and then when the theater was full he'd go inside and start beating a drum. Bumbuku would come out and dance and do all sorts of acrobatics. But the trick that pleased people most of all was when Bumbuku would walk across a tight rope, carrying a paper parasol in one hand and a fan in the other. The people thought this most wonderful. They would cheer and cheer for Bumbuku. And after every show the junkman would give Bumbuku some delicious rice-cakes to eat.

The junkman sold so many tickets that he finally became extremely rich. One day he said to Bumbuku: "You must get very tired doing these tricks every day. I now have all the money I need. So why don't I take you back to the temple, where you can live very quietly?"

"Well," said Bumbuku, "I *am* getting a little tired and I *would* like to live quietly in a temple. But that old priest might put me on the fire again, and he might never give me delicious rice-cakes."

"Just leave everything to me," the junkman said.

So the next morning the junkman took Bumbuku and a large amount of money and some of Bumbuku's favorite rice-cakes to the temple.

When they got to the temple the junkman explained to the priest everything that had happened, and he gave all the money to the priest for the temple. Then he said: "So will you please let Bumbuku live here quietly forever, always feeding him rice-cakes like these I've brought and never putting him over the fire?"

23

"Indeed I will," said the priest. "He shall have the honored place in the temple's treasure house. It's really a magic kettle of good luck, and I would never have put it over the fire if only I'd known."

So the priest called his pupils. They put the kettle on a wooden stand, and the rice-cakes on another stand. Then, with the priest carrying one stand, and the junkman carrying the other, and the three pupils following after, they carried Bumbuku carefully to the treasure house, and put the rice-cakes beside him.

It is said that Bumbuku is still there in the treasure house of the temple today, where he is very happy. They still give him delicious rice-cakes to eat every day and never, never put him over a fire. He is peaceful. He is happy.

Monkey-Dance and Sparrow-Dance

ONCE there was an old woodcutter who went so far into the mountains to find wood that he got lost. He walked for a long time, not knowing where he was going, until he suddenly heard music in the distance and smelled the odors of food and drink.

Climbing up to the top of a hill, he saw a great crowd of monkeys. They were eating and dancing and singing, and drinking a kind of wine that they had made from rice. It smelled so good that the old man at once wanted some.

They sang and danced beautifully, much to the old man's surprise. Then one monkey took up a bottle made from a gourd, filled it with wine, and said it was time for him to be going home. The other monkeys told him goodbye and he started home. When the old man saw this, he decided to follow the monkey and see if he couldn't get some of the wine for himself.

Before long the gourd-bottle grew very heavy. So the monkey stopped and poured some of the wine into a jar. He hid the gourd with the rest of the wine in the hollow of an old tree, put the jar on his head, and went merrily on his way, balancing the jar carefully.

The old man had been peeping and had seen all this. When the monkey was gone, the old man said: "Surely he won't mind if I just borrow some of that wonderful wine." So he ran to the hollow tree, and filled a jar with some of the wine. "This is wonderful," he thought. "If it tastes as good as it smells, it must be very fine indeed. I'll take this back to my wife—if I can find my way home."

In the meantime his wife was having an adventure too. She was washing clothes under a tree and suddenly noticed that the sparrows were having a kind of party. They too were drinking something that smelled so good the old woman just had to have some.

So, when the sparrows had finished dancing and singing, the old woman quickly tucked one of their gourd-bottles under her robe and hurried home. "I'll take this to my husband," she thought, "for if it tastes as good as it smells, it must be fine indeed."

No sooner had she arrived than her husband appeared, having finally found his way home. "I have something to show you," they both said at the same time. And then, one by one, they told each other their stories. Then they exchanged their bottles and drank the wine.

It tasted delicious, but no sooner had they drunk it than they both felt an uncontrollable desire to dance and sing. The old woman began to chatter and jump around like a monkey, while the old man held his hands out and chirped like a sparrow.

First the old man sang:

"One hundred sparrows dance in the spring!
Chirp-a chirp, chirp-a chirp, ching!"

Then the old lady sang:

"One hundred monkeys making a clatter.
Chatter-chat, chatter-chat, chatter."

They made so much noise that the man who owned the woods they lived in heard them and came running. There he saw the old woman dancing and acting like a monkey, and the old man dancing and acting like a sparrow. "Here, here!" he said. "This will never do. If you're going to dance, a woman's dance should be graceful and lady-like, like a sparrow's dance, and a man's dance should be bold and manly, like a monkey's dance. Not the other way around."

So the old couple stopped dancing and told their landlord the stories of their adventures. "Well, of course," he said, "you've each been drinking the wrong wine. Why don't you change bottles again and see what happens."

After that the old man always drank the monkey wine, and danced in a very manly way. And the old woman always drank the sparrow wine, and danced in a very lady-like way. Everyone who saw them dance and heard their songs thought them very lovely and started imitating them. And that is why to this day a man leaps about nimbly and boldly when he dances, while a woman is much more graceful and bird-like when she dances.

The Long-Nosed Goblins

LONG ago there were two long-nosed goblins who lived in the high mountains of northern Japan. One was a blue goblin and the other was a red goblin. They were both very proud of their noses, which they could extend for many, many leagues across the countryside, and they were always arguing as to which had the most beautiful nose.

One day the blue goblin was resting on top of a mountain when he smelled a very good smell coming from somewhere down on the plains. "My, but something smells good," he said. "Wonder what it is."

So he started extending his nose, letting it grow longer and longer as it followed the good smell. His nose grew so long that it crossed seven mountains, went down into the plains, and finally ended up at a lord's mansion.

Inside the mansion the lord's daughter, Princess White-flower, was having a party. Many other little princesses had come to the party, and Princess White-flower was showing them all her rare and beautiful dress materials. They had opened the treasure house and taken out the wonderful pieces of cloth, all packed in incense. It was the incense that the blue goblin had smelled.

Just at that moment the princess was looking for some place to hang the cloth up so they could see it better. When she caught sight of the blue goblin's nose, she said: "Oh, look, someone's hung a blue pole on the terrace. We'll hang the cloth on it."

So the princess called her maids and they hung the pieces of beautiful cloth on the goblin's nose. The blue goblin, sitting way back on his mountain, felt something tickling his nose, so he began pulling it back in.

When the princesses saw the beautiful pieces of cloth go flying away through the air, they were very surprised. They tried to catch the cloth, but they were too late.

When the blue goblin saw the beautiful cloth hanging on his nose, he was very pleased. He gathered the cloth up and took it home with him. Then he invited the red goblin, who lived on the next mountain, to come and see him.

"Just look what a wonderful nose I have," he said to the red goblin. "It brought me all this wonderful cloth."

The red goblin was jealous when he saw this. He would have turned green with envy except that red goblins can't turn green.

"I'll show you my nose is still the best," the red goblin said. "Just you wait and I'll show you."

After that the red goblin sat up on top of his mountain every day, rubbing his long red nose and sniffing the air. Many days passed and he still hadn't smelled any incense. He became very impatient and said: "Well, I won't wait any longer. I'll send my nose down to the plains anyway, and it's sure to find something good there."

So the red goblin started extending his nose, letting it grow longer and longer, until it crossed seven mountains, down into the plains, and finally ended up at the same lord's mansion.

Just at that moment the lord's son, Prince Valorous, and his little friends were playing in the garden. When Prince Valorous caught sight of the red goblin's nose, he cried, "Just look at this red pole that someone's put here. Let's swing on it."

33

So they got some thick ropes and tied them onto the red pole and made several swings. Then how they played! Several of the boys would get in the same swing and they'd swing high up toward the sky. They climbed all over the red pole, jumped up and down on it, and one even began to cut his initials in the pole with a knife.

How all this hurt the red goblin, sitting back on his mountain! His nose was so heavy that he couldn't move it. But when the boy started cutting on it, the red goblin pulled with all his might and shook all the boys off his nose. Then he pulled it back to his mountain as fast as he could.

The blue goblin laughed and laughed at the sight. But the red goblin only sat stroking his nose and saying: "This is what I get for being jealous of other people. I'm never going to send my nose down into the plains again."

The Rabbit in the Moon

ONCE the Old-Man-of-the-Moon looked down into a big forest on the earth. He saw a rabbit and a monkey and a fox all living there together in the forest as very good friends.

"Now, I wonder which of them is the kindest," he said to himself. "I think I'll go down and see."

So the old man changed himself into a beggar and came down from the moon to the forest where the three animals were.

"Please help me," he said to them. "I'm very, very hungry."

"Oh! what a poor old beggar!" they said, and then they went hurrying off to find some food for the beggar.

The monkey brought a lot of fruit. And the fox caught a big fish. But the rabbit couldn't find anything at all to bring.

"Oh my! oh my! what shall I do?" the rabbit cried. But just then he got an idea.

"Please, Mr. Monkey," the rabbit said, "you gather some firewood for me. And you, Mr. Fox, please make a big fire with the wood."

They did as the rabbit asked, and when the fire was burning very brightly, the rabbit said to the beggar: "I don't have anything to give you. So I'll put myself in this fire, and then when I'm cooked you can eat me."

The rabbit was about to jump into the fire and cook himself. But just then the beggar suddenly changed himself back into the Old-Man-of-the-Moon.

"You're very kind, Mr. Rabbit," the Old Man said. "But you should never do anything to harm yourself. Since you're the kindest of all, I'll take you home to live with me."

Then the Old-Man-of-the-Moon took the rabbit in his arms and carried him up to the moon. Just look and see! If you look carefully at the moon when it is shining brightly, you can still see the rabbit there where the old man put him so very long ago.

The Tongue-Cut Sparrow

THERE was once an old man who had a very mean wife, with a terrible temper. They didn't have any children, so the old man made a pet out of a tiny sparrow. He took very good care of the little bird, and when he came home from work every day he would pet and talk to it until suppertime, and then feed it with food from his own plate. He treated the sparrow just as if it were his own child.

But the old woman wouldn't ever show any kindness to anyone or anything. She particularly hated the sparrow and was always scolding her husband for keeping such a nuisance around the house. Her temper was particularly bad on wash days, because she very much disliked hard work.

One day while the old man was gone to his work in the fields, the wife was getting ready to wash the clothes. She had made some starch and set it out in a wooden bowl to cool. While her back was turned, the sparrow hopped down onto the edge of the bowl and pecked at some of the starch. Just then the woman turned around and saw what the sparrow was doing. She became so angry that she grabbed up a pair of scissors—and cut the sparrow's tongue right off! Then she threw the sparrow into the air, crying: "Now get away from here, you nasty little bird!" So the poor sparrow went flying away into the woods.

A little while later the old man came home and found the sparrow gone. He looked and looked for his pet, and kept asking his wife about it. She finally told him what she had done. He felt very sorry about it, and the next morning he started out into the forest to look for the sparrow. He kept calling: "Where are you, little sparrow? Where are you, little sparrow?"

Suddenly the sparrow came flying up to the old man. It was all dressed in the kimono of a beautiful woman, and it could speak with a human voice. "Hello, my dear master," the sparrow said. "You must be very tired, so please come to my house and rest."

When the old man heard the sparrow speaking, he knew it must be a fairy sparrow. He followed the sparrow and soon came to a beautiful house in the forest. The sparrow led him into the house and into the parlor. The sparrow had many daughters, and they brought a feast for the old man, giving him many, many wonderful things to eat and drink. Four of the daughters did a beautiful Sparrow Dance. They danced so gracefully that the old man kept clapping and clapping, begging them to keep on dancing.

Before he realized it, the sun began to set. When he saw that it was getting dark he jumped up and said he must hurry home because his wife would be worried about him. The sparrow begged him to stay longer, and he was having such a good time that he hated to leave. But still he said: "No, I really must go."

"Well, then," said the sparrow, "let me give you a gift to take home with you."

The sparrow brought out two baskets, one big and heavy and one small and light. "Please take your choice," the sparrow said.

The old man didn't want to be greedy, so he took the small basket and started for home. When he got home, he told his wife everything that had happened. Then they opened the basket. It was full of all sorts of wonderful things—gold and silver, diamonds and rubies, coral and money bags. There was enough in the basket to make them rich all the rest of their lives.

The old man was very glad when he saw this treasure. But the old woman became very angry. "You fool!" she said. "Why didn't you choose the big basket? Then we would have had much more. I'm going to the sparrow's house myself and get the other basket."

The old man begged her not to be so greedy, saying that they already had enough. But the old woman was determined. She put on her straw sandals and started off.

When she reached the sparrow's house, she spoke very sweetly to the sparrow. The sparrow invited her into the house and gave her some tea

and cookies. When the old woman started to leave, the sparrow again brought out one big basket and one small basket and told the woman to choose one as a gift. The old woman quickly grabbed the big basket. It was so heavy she could hardly get it on her back, but with the sparrow's help she lifted it up and started home.

Along the way the basket got heavier and heavier. The old woman kept wondering what wonderful things were inside the basket. Finally she sat down to rest beside the road, and her curiosity got the better of her. She just had to open the basket! When she did, all sorts of terrible things jumped out at her. There was a devil's head that made frightening noises at her, and a wasp that came flying at her with a long stinger, and snakes and toads and slimy things. How frightened she was!

She jumped up and went running home as fast as she could. She told the old man what had happened. Then she said: "I promise never to be mean or greedy again." And it seems she had actually learned her lesson, because ever after that she was very kind and always helped the old man feed any birds that came flying into their garden.

Silly Saburo

LONG ago there was a boy who lived on a farm in Japan. His name was Saburo, but he always did such silly things that people called him Silly Saburo. He could never remember more than one thing at a time, and then would do that one thing, no matter how silly it might be. His father and mother were very worried about him, but they hoped he'd get smarter as he grew older, and they were always very patient with him.

45

One day his father said: "Saburo, please go to the potato patch today and dig up the potatoes. After you've dug them up, spread them out carefully and leave them to dry in the sun."

"I understand," said Saburo. So he put his hoe over his shoulder and went out to the potato patch.

Saburo was busy digging the potatoes when all of a sudden his hoe hit something in the earth. He dug deeper and found a big old pot. When he looked inside the pot he found it was filled with large gold coins. It was a huge treasure that someone had buried there long ago.

"Father said I must first dig things up and then leave them to dry in the sun," Saburo said to himself. So he very carefully spread the gold coins out. Then he went home and said: "I found a pot of gold and spread the gold in the sun to dry."

His parents were very surprised when they heard this. They went running to the potato patch, but someone had taken all the gold. There was

not a single coin left. "Next time you find something," his father said, "you must wrap it up very carefully and bring it home. Now don't forget!"

"I understand," said Saburo. And the next day he found a dead cat in the field. So he wrapped it up very carefully and brought it home, very proud of having remembered.

His father said: "Don't be so silly. When you find something like this, . you must throw it in the river."

Next day Saburo dug up a huge tree stump. He thought very hard and remembered what his father had said about the dead cat. So he took the stump and threw it with a great splash in the river.

Just then a neighbor was passing. "You mustn't throw away valuable things like that," the neighbor said. "That stump would have made good firewood. You should have broken it up into small pieces and taken it home."

"I understand," said Saburo, and started on his way home. On his way home he saw a teacup which somebody had left beside the road. "Oh, here's a valuable thing!" said Saburo. So he took his hoe and broke the teapot and teacup up into very small pieces. Then he gathered up the pieces and took them home with him.

"Hello, Mother," he said. "Look what I found and brought home." Then he showed his mother the broken pieces of china.

"Oh, my!" said his mother. "That's the teapot and teacup that I took to your father with his lunch this noon. And you've completely ruined them!"

Next day his parents said: "Everything you do, you do wrong. We'll go out into the fields and work today. You stay home and keep the house." So they left Saburo alone.

"I really don't understand why people call me Silly Saburo," he said to himself. "I do everything just exactly the way people tell me to do."

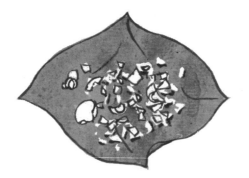

The Toothpick Warriors

ONCE upon a time there was a princess who had a very bad habit. She would lie in bed at night and pick her teeth with a toothpick. That wasn't so bad, but after she was done, instead of throwing the toothpick away as she should have, she would stick it between the straw mats that make the floor of a Japanese house and upon which the princess slept. Now, this was not a very clean habit, and since the princess did this every night the cracks between the mats were soon filled with used toothpicks.

One night she was suddenly awakened by the noise of fighting. She heard the voices of warriors and the sound of swords. Frightened, she sat up and lit the lamp beside her bed. She was so surprised by what she saw that she could hardly believe her eyes:

There, right beside her quilts, were many tiny little warriors. Some were fighting, some were singing, some were dancing, and all were making a great deal of noise.

The princess thought that she must be dreaming, so she pinched herself. But, no, she was wide awake, and the tiny warriors were still there making a terrible racket. They made so much noise that she couldn't sleep at all that night, and when she did manage to doze off, she suddenly woke up because it was so quiet. The tiny warriors had left.

She was very afraid, but she was ashamed to tell the lord, her father, because he probably wouldn't have believed her. Yet, next night when she went to bed, the same thing happened again, and the night after that too.

The tiny warriors made so much noise every night that she couldn't sleep, and each day the princess became a little paler than the day before. Soon she became very ill from lack of sleep.

Her father kept asking her what the matter was, and finally she told him. At first he didn't believe her, but finally he decided to see for himself. He told her that she should sleep in his room and he would stand watch in hers.

And so he did. But though he remained awake all night long and watched and waited, the tiny warriors did not come. While waiting, however, he noticed the many toothpicks lying about on the floor. He looked very

carefully at the toothpicks and finally discovered what had been happening.

Next day he called his daughter to him and showed her one of the toothpicks. Its sides were all scarred and cut. The marks were so very tiny that the princess could just barely see them. She asked her father what the marks meant.

Her father explained that the tiny warriors had come to her room because she left toothpicks lying around. They had no swords of their own and wanted some very much. Now, for a tiny warrior, a toothpick made the best possible kind of sword, and that was the reason they came every night.

They hadn't come last night, he said, because he was there with a real sword, and they were afraid. Then he looked at his daughter sternly and asked her why there were so many used toothpicks in her room.

The princess was very ashamed of her bad habit but admitted that she had used the toothpicks and stuck them between the cracks of the mats because she was too lazy to get up and throw them away properly. She also said she was very, very sorry and promised that she would never, never be so lazy again.

Then she picked up all the toothpicks, even those that were at the very bottom of the cracks, and threw them all away. That night the warriors did not come because there were no tiny swords for them. And they never came again.

Soon the princess became healthy again because the warriors no longer kept her awake. She became very neat about everything, and pleased her father greatly by even sweeping the garden every day. She never forgot the tiny warriors, and if she ever used a toothpick again, you may be sure she was very careful to throw it away properly.

The Sticky-Sticky Pine

ONCE there was a woodcutter. He was very poor but very kind. Never would he tear off the living branches of a tree to make firewood. Instead, he would gather only the dead branches on the ground. He knew what happened when you tore a branch off a tree. The sap, which is the blood of a tree, would drip and drip, just as though the poor tree were bleeding. So, since he didn't want to harm the trees, he never tore off the branches.

55

One day he was walking beneath a high pine tree hunting for firewood when he heard a voice, saying:

"Sticky, sticky is my sap,
For my tender twigs are snapped."

The woodcutter looked and, sure enough, someone had broken three limbs off the pine and the sap was running out. Skillfully, he mended them, saying:

"Now these tender twigs I'll wrap,
And in that way stop the sap."

And he tore a piece from his own clothes to make a bandage.

No sooner had he finished than many tiny gold and silver things fell from the tree. It was money—a lot of it. The surprised woodcutter was

almost covered up with it. He looked at the tree and smiled and thanked it. Then he took the money home.

There was a great amount and he slowly realized that he was now a very rich woodcutter indeed. Everyone knows that the pine tree is the sign of prosperity in Japan and, sure enough, the grateful pine had made him very rich.

Just then a face appeared in the window. It was the face of another woodcutter. But this woodcutter was neither nice nor kind. In fact, it was he who had torn off the branches of the pine and had broken its twigs. When he saw the money he said: "Where did you get all that money? Look how nice and bright it is."

The good woodcutter held up the money so the other could see. It was oblong in shape, the way money used to be in Japan, and he had five basketfuls. He told the bad woodcutter how he had got the money.

"From that big pine tree?"

"Yes, that was the one."

"Hmm," said the bad woodcutter and ran away as fast as he could go. He ran right up to the old pine tree, and the tree said:

"Sticky, sticky, is my blood.
Touch me, you'll receive a flood."

"Oh, just what I want," said the bad man, "a flood of gold and silver." He reached up and broke off another branch. The pine tree suddenly showered him. But it showered him with sticky, sticky sap—not gold and silver at all.

The bad woodcutter was covered with sap. It got in his hair and on his arms and legs. Since it was so sticky, he couldn't move and though he called for help, no one could hear him. He had to remain there for three days— one day for each branch—until the sap became soft enough for him to drag himself home.

And, after that, he never broke another branch off a living tree.

The Spider Weaver

LONG ago there was a young farmer named Yosaku. One day he was working in the fields and saw a snake getting ready to eat a spider. Yosaku felt very sorry for the spider. So he ran at the snake with his hoe and drove the snake away, thus saving the spider's life. Then the spider disappeared into the grass, but first it seemed to pause a minute and bow in thanks toward Yosaku.

One morning not long after that, Yosaku was in his house when he heard a tiny voice outside calling: "Mr. Yosaku, Mr. Yosaku." He went to the door and saw a beautiful young girl standing in the yard.

"I heard that you are looking for someone to weave cloth for you," said the girl. "Won't you please let me live here and weave for you?"

Yosaku was very pleased because he did need a weaving girl. So he showed the girl the weaving room and she started to work at the loom. At the end of the day Yosaku went to see what she'd done and was very surprised to find that she'd woven eight long pieces of cloth, enough to make eight kimono. He'd never known anyone could weave so much in just a single day.

"How ever did you weave so much?" he asked the girl.

But instead of answering him, she said a very strange thing: "You mustn't ask me that. And you must never come into the weaving room while I am at work."

But Yosaku was very curious. So one day he slipped very quietly up to the weaving room and peeped in the window. What he saw really surprised him! Because it was not the girl who was seated at the loom, but a large spider, weaving very fast with its eight legs, and for thread it was using its own spider web, which came out of its mouth.

Yosaku looked very closely and saw that it was the same spider which he'd saved from the snake. Then Yosaku understood. The spider had been so thankful that it had wanted to do something to help Yosaku. So it had turned itself into a beautiful young girl and come to weave cloth for him. Just by eating the cotton in the weaving room it could spin it into thread

inside its own body, and then with its eight legs it could weave the thread into cloth very, very fast.

Yosaku was very grateful for the spider's help. He saw that the cotton was almost used up. So next morning he set out for the nearest village, on the other side of the mountains, to buy some more cotton. He bought a big bundle of cotton and started home, carrying it on his back.

Along the way a very terrible thing happened. Yosaku sat down to rest, and the same snake that he'd driven away from the spider came up and slipped inside the bundle of cotton. But Yosaku didn't know anything about this. So he carried the cotton home and gave it to the weaving girl.

She was very glad to get the cotton, because she'd now used up all the cotton that was left. So she took it and went to the weaving room.

As soon as the girl was inside the weaving room she turned back into a spider and began eating the cotton very, very fast, just as though it were something very delicious, so she could spin it into thread inside her body. The spider ate and ate and ate, and then suddenly, when it had eaten down to the bottom of the bundle—the snake jumped out of the cotton. It opened its mouth wide to swallow the spider. The spider was very frightened and jumped out of the window. The snake went wriggling very fast after it. And the spider had eaten so much cotton that it couldn't run very fast. So the snake gradually caught up with the spider. Again the snake opened its mouth wide to gulp the spider down. But just then a wonderful thing happened.

Old Man Sun, up in the sky, had been watching what was happening. He knew how kind the spider had been to Yosaku and he felt very sorry

for the poor little spider. So he reached down with a sunbeam and caught hold of the end of the web that was sticking out of the spider's mouth, and he lifted the spider high up into the sky, where the snake couldn't reach it at all.

The spider was very grateful to Old Man Sun for saving him from the snake. So he used all the cotton that was inside his body to weave beautiful fleecy clouds up in the sky. That's the reason, they say, why clouds are soft and white like cotton, and also that is the reason why both a spider and a cloud are called by the same name in Japan—*kumo*.

Little One-Inch

THERE was once a married couple who had no children. One day they went to a shrine and prayed, saying: "Oh, please give us a child. We want a child so very badly." On their way home they heard a tiny crying sound coming from a clump of grass. They looked in the grass, and there they found a tiny little baby boy, wrapped in a bright red blanket. "This is the child that has come in answer to our prayers," they said. So they took the little baby home with them and raised him as their own son.

Now this baby was so tiny that he wasn't as large as a person's thumb, and even as he grew older he stayed the same size. He was just about an inch tall, so they named him Little One-Inch.

One day, when he had grown older, Little One-Inch said to his parents: "I thank you very much for raising me so carefully. But now I must go out into the world and make my fortune."

They tried to keep him from going, saying he was too tiny to go out into the world. But he insisted, so finally his parents said: "All right, we'll get you ready for the journey." So they gave him a needle to use as a sword, a wooden bowl to use as a boat, and a chopstick to use as an oar.

Little One-Inch got in his boat and waved goodbye to his parents, promising to come back when he'd made his fortune. Then he went floating down the river in his rice-bowl boat, paddling with his chopstick.

He floated for many, many miles, and then suddenly his boat was turned over. It was a frog in the river that had hit the boat. Little One-Inch was a very good swimmer. He swam to the bank and found himself standing before a great lord's house.

Little One-Inch looked at the house and saw that it must belong to a very wealthy lord. So he walked boldly up to the front door and called out. A manservant came to the door, but he couldn't see anyone.

"Here I am, down here," cried Little One-Inch. "Look down here."

The servant looked down at the floor by the front door. At first all he saw was the pair of wooden sandals that the lord used when he went out walking. Then the servant looked closer and saw the tiny figure of Little One-Inch standing beside the sandals. He was so surprised that he hurried off to tell the lord.

The lord came to the front door himself and looked at Little One-Inch, who was standing there very proudly, with his needle-sword at his hip.

"Why, hello there, little knight," said the lord. "What do you want here?"

"I've come out into the world to seek my fortune," said Little One-Inch. "And if you'll have me, I pray that you let me become one of your guards. I may be small, but I can fight very well with this fine sword I have."

The lord was very amused to hear a tiny boy use such bold words. "All right, all right," he said, "you can come and be a playmate for my daughter, the princess."

So after that Little One-Inch became the constant companion of the princess. They became very good friends, reading books and playing together every day. The princess made a bed for Little One-Inch in one of her jewel boxes.

One day the princess and Little One-Inch went to visit a temple near the lord's house. Suddenly a terrible green devil appeared, carrying a magic hammer. When the devil saw the princess he started trying to catch her. Little One-Inch drew his sword and began sticking the devil's toes with it. But the devil's skin was so thick that the tiny needle-sword wouldn't even go through it. The devil was getting nearer and nearer to the princess. So Little One-Inch climbed up the devil's body and out onto his arm. Then he waved the sword at the devil's nose. This made the devil so angry that he opened his mouth wide to give a big roar.

At that moment Little One-Inch gave a big leap and jumped right into the devil's mouth. Then he began cutting the devil's tongue with his sword. Now the devil's tongue was very tender and the needle hurt very much. He was so surprised at this that he spit Little One-Inch out onto the ground and went running away. He even dropped his magic hammer.

The princess ran and picked up the magic hammer. "Now we can make a wish," she said. Then she shook the hammer in the air and said: "Please let Little One-Inch grow taller."

And, sure enough, each time the princess shook the hammer Little One-Inch grew one inch taller. She kept right on shaking it until Little One-Inch was just as tall as she was. They were both very happy about this, and the lord was happy too when he heard what had happened.

When they were a few years older Little One-Inch and the princess were married and they lived very happily ever after.

The Badger and the Magic Fan

IN JAPAN goblins are called *tengu* and they all have very long noses. Now once upon a time three tengu children were playing in the forest. They had a magic fan. When they fanned their noses with one side of the fan, their noses would grow longer and longer, and when they fanned with the other side, their noses would shrink back to the original size. They were having a wonderful time fanning their noses back and forth.

Just then a badger came by and saw what they were doing. "My! how I'd like to have a fan like that!" he said to himself. And then he thought of a good trick. Because, you see, badgers are always playing tricks and can change themselves into any shape they want. So the badger changed himself into the shape of a little girl. He took a plate of bean-jam buns and went to the tengu children.

"Hello, little tengu children," said the badger. "I've brought you some wonderful bean-jam buns. Please let me play with you."

The tengu children were delighted, because they loved to eat bean-jam buns. But there were four buns to be divided among the three of them. And they immediately started arguing over who was to get the extra bun.

Finally the badger said: "I tell you what let's do. You all close your eyes, and the one who can keep his eyes closed and hold his breath the longest will win the extra bun."

They all agreed to this. The badger counted "One! Two! Three!" and the tengu children closed their eyes hard. As soon as they did this the badger grabbed up the magic fan and went running away with it as fast as he could, leaving the tengu children still holding their breath and keeping their eyes closed.

"Ha, ha, ha," laughed the badger. "I certainly made fools out of those tengu children."

The badger went on walking toward the city. Presently he came to a temple. At the temple he saw a beautiful girl dressed in very expensive clothes. He felt sure she was the daughter of a wealthy man, and in fact her father was the richest man in the country. So the badger crept up behind her on tiptoe. Quick as a flash he fanned her nose with the magic fan. Instantly her nose grew a yard long!

What a terrible to-do there was! Here was the beautiful little rich girl with a nose a yard long! Her father called all the doctors in the country,

but none of them could do anything to make her nose short. Her father spent much money on medicines, but nothing did any good. Finally in desperation the father said: "I'll give my daughter as a wife and half my fortune to anyone who can make her nose grow short again."

When the badger heard this, he said: "That's what I've been waiting for." He quickly went to the girl's house and announced he'd come to fix her nose. So the father took the badger to the girl's room. The badger took out the magic fan and fanned her nose with the other side of it. In the twinkling of an eye her nose was short again!

Her father was very happy and started making preparations for the wedding. The badger was very happy too because he was not only going to get a beautiful wife, but also a large fortune. On the day of the wedding there was a great feast. The badger was so happy that he ate and drank much too much and became very hot and sleepy.

Without thinking what he was doing, he lay back on some pillows, closed his eyes, and began fanning himself with the magic fan. Immediately his nose began to grow longer and longer. But he was half asleep and didn't see what was happening. So he kept on fanning and fanning and his nose kept on growing and growing. It went right up through the ceiling and on high up into the sky until it pierced the clouds.

Now, up above the clouds there were some heavenly workers building a bridge across the Milky Way. "Look at that!" they yelled, pointing to the badger's nose. "There's a pole just the right size for our bridge. Come, let's pull it up."

So they all began pulling on the badger's nose. How this surprised the badger! He started up out of his sleep, crying: "Ouch! Ouch! Help! Help!" And he began to fan his nose with the other side of the fan as hard as he could.

But it was too late. The workers kept on pulling him up, yelling: "Heave ho! Heave ho!" They pulled him all the way up into the sky, and no one ever saw him again.

Mr. Lucky Straw

ONCE upon a time, long ago, there was a young man named Shobei who lived in a farm village in Japan.

One day on his way home from working in the fields he tripped on a stone and tumbled over and over on the ground. When he stopped tumbling he discovered that he had caught a piece of straw up in his hand.

"Well, well," he said, "a piece of straw is a worthless thing, but it seems I was meant to pick this one up, so I won't throw it away."

As he went walking along, holding the straw in his hand, a dragonfly came flying in circles around his head.

"What a pest!" he said, "I'll show this dragonfly not to bother me!" So he caught the dragonfly and tied the straw around its tail.

He went on walking, holding the dragonfly, and presently met a woman walking with her little boy.

When the little boy saw the dragonfly, he wanted it very badly. "Mother, please get me that dragonfly," he said. "Please, please, *please!*"

"Here, little boy, I'll give you the dragonfly," Shobei said, handing the boy the straw.

To express her appreciation, the boy's mother gave Shobei three of the oranges she was carrying.

Shobei thanked her and went on his way. Before long he met a peddler who was so thirsty that he was almost fainting. There was no water anywhere near. Shobei felt very sorry for the peddler and gave him all the oranges, so he could drink the juice.

The peddler was very grateful, and in exchange he gave Shobei three pieces of cloth.

Shobei went on his way, carrying the cloth, and met a princess riding in a fine carriage guarded by many attendants.

The princess looked out of the carriage at Shobei and said: "Oh, what pretty cloth you have there. Please let me have it."

Shobei gave the princess the cloth and, to thank him, she gave him a large sum of money.

Shobei took the money and bought many fields with it. He divided the fields up among the people of his village. Thus everyone had a piece of land of his own. They all worked very hard in their fields. The village became very prosperous and many new barns and storehouses were built. Everyone was amazed when they remembered that all this wealth came from the little straw which Shobei had happened to pick up.

Shobei became the most important man in the village. Everyone respected him greatly. And as long as he lived they all called him "Mr. Lucky Straw."

Mr. Lucky Straw

Why the Jellyfish Has No Bones

LONG ago all the sea creatures lived happily in the palace of the Dragon King, deep at the bottom of the sea—well, almost happily. The only enemies were the octopus, who was the palace doctor, and the jellyfish, who back then had bones like all the other sea creatures.

One day the daughter of the Dragon King became sick. The octopus came to see her and said she would die unless she had some medicine made from the liver of a monkey. "The jellyfish can swim very fast," the octopus

said to the king, "so why don't you send him to get a monkey's liver?"
So the king called the jellyfish and sent him on the errand.

But finding a monkey's liver wasn't easy. Even finding a monkey was
difficult. The jellyfish swam and swam and swam. Finally one day near a
little island he found a monkey who had fallen in the sea.

"Help! Help!" called the monkey, who could not swim.

"I'll help you," said the jellyfish, "but you must promise to give me
your liver to make medicine for the Dragon King's daughter." The
monkey promised; so the jellyfish took him on his back and went swim-
ming away very fast toward the palace.

The monkey had been willing to promise anything while he was drown-
ing, but now that he was safe he began thinking about it. And the more
he thought the less he liked the idea of giving up his liver, even for the
Dragon King's daughter. No, he decided, he didn't like the idea one little
bit.

84   *Why the Jellyfish Has No Bones*

Being a very clever monkey, he said: "Wait a minute! Wait a minute! I just remembered that I left my liver hanging in a pine tree on the island. Take me back there and I'll get it."

So they returned to the island and the monkey climbed a high pine tree. Then he called out to the jellyfish: "Thank you very much for saving me. I can't find my liver anywhere, so I'll just stay here, thank you."

The jellyfish realized he'd been tricked. But there was nothing he could do about it. He swam slowly back to the palace at the bottom of the sea and told what had happened. The king was very angry.

"Let me and the other fish beat this no-good fellow for you," said the octopus.

"All right, beat him hard," said the King.

So they beat him and beat him until all his bones were broken. He cried and cried, and the wicked octopus laughed and laughed.

Just then the princess came running in. "Look!" she cried, "I'm not sick at all. I just had a little stomach-ache."

The octopus had planned all this so he could get even with his enemy, the jellyfish. The Dragon King became so furious that he sent the octopus away from the palace forever and made the jellyfish his favorite. So this is why the octopus now lives alone, scorned and feared by all who live in the sea. And this is why, even though he still has no bones and can no longer swim fast, the jellyfish is never bothered by the other creatures of the sea.

The Old Man Who Made Trees Blossom

ONCE upon a time there was a very kind old man and his wife living in a certain village. Next door to them lived a very mean old man and his wife. The kind old couple had a little white dog named Shiro. They loved Shiro very much and always gave him good things to eat. But the mean old man hated dogs, and every time he saw Shiro he threw stones at him.

87

One day Shiro began barking very loudly out in the farmyard. The kind old man went out to see what was the matter. Shiro kept barking and barking and began digging in the ground. "Oh, you want me to help you dig?" asked the old man. So he brought a spade and began digging. Suddenly his spade hit something hard. He kept digging and found a large pot full of many pieces of gold money. Then he thanked Shiro very much for leading him to so much gold, and took the money to his house.

Now the mean old man had been peeping and had seen all this. He wanted some gold too. So the next day he asked the kind old man if he could borrow Shiro for a little while. "Why, of course you may borrow Shiro, if he'll be of any help to you," said the kind old man.

The mean old man took Shiro to his house and out into his field. "Now find me some gold too," he ordered the dog, "or I'll beat you." So Shiro began digging at a certain spot. Then the mean old man tied

Shiro up and began digging himself. But all he found in the hole was some terrible smelling garbage—no gold at all. This made him so angry that he hit Shiro over the head with his spade, and killed him.

The kind old man and woman were very sad about Shiro. They buried him in their field and planted a little pine tree over his grave. And every day they went to Shiro's grave and watered the pine tree very carefully. The tree began to grow very fast, and in only few years it became very big. The kind old woman said: "Remember how Shiro used to love to eat rice-cakes? Let's cut down that big pine tree and make a mortar. Then with the mortar we'll make some rice-cakes in memory of Shiro."

So the old man cut down the tree and made a mortar out of its trunk. Then they filled it full of steamed rice and began pounding the rice to make rice-cakes. But no sooner did the old man began pounding than all

the rice turned into gold! Now the kind old man and woman were richer than ever.

The mean old man had been peeping through the window and had seen the rice turn to gold. He still wanted some gold for himself very badly. So the next day he came and asked if he could borrow the mortar. "Why, of course you may borrow the mortar," said the kind old man.

The mean old man took the mortar home and filled it full of steamed rice. "Now watch," he said to his wife. "When I begin pounding this rice, it'll turn to gold." But when he began pounding, the rice turned to terrible smelling garbage, and there was no gold at all. This made him so angry that he got his ax and cut the mortar up into small pieces and burned it up in the stove.

When the kind old man went to get his mortar back, it was all burned to ashes. He was very sad, because the mortar had reminded him of Shiro. So he asked for some of the ashes and took them home with him.

It was the middle of winter and all the trees were bare. He thought he'd scatter some of the ashes around in his garden. When he did, all the cherry trees in the garden suddenly began to bloom right in the middle of winter. Everybody came to see this wonderful sight, and the prince who lived in a nearby castle heard about it.

Now this prince had a cherry tree in his garden that he loved very much. He could hardly wait for spring to come so he could see the beautiful blossoms on this cherry tree. But when spring came he discovered that the tree was dead and he felt very sad. So he sent for the kind old man and asked him to bring the tree back to life. The old man took some

The Old Man Who Made Trees Blossom

of the ashes and climbed the tree. Then he threw the ashes up into the dead branches, and almost more quickly than you can think, the tree was covered with the most beautiful blossoms it had ever had.

The prince had come on horseback to watch and he was very pleased. He gave the kind old man a great deal of gold and many presents. And, best of all, he knighted the old man and gave him a new name, "Sir Old-Man-Who-Makes-Trees-Blossom."

Sir Old-Man-Who-Makes-Trees-Blossom and his wife were now very rich, and they lived very happily for many more years.

The Crab and the Monkey

ONCE a crab and a monkey went for a walk together. Along the way the monkey found a persimmon seed, and the crab found a rice-ball. The monkey wanted the crab's rice-ball, and being a very clever talker, he finally persuaded the crab to trade the rice-ball for the persimmon seed. The monkey quickly ate the rice-ball.

The crab couldn't eat the persimmon seed, but he took it home and planted it in his garden, where it began to grow. Because the crab tended it carefully every day, it grew and grew.

94

The tiny seed finally became a big tree, and then one autumn the crab saw that it was full of beautiful persimmons. The crab wanted very much to eat the persimmons, but no matter how hard he tried, he couldn't climb the tree. So he asked his friend the monkey to pick the persimmons for him. Now, the monkey loved persimmons even better than rice-balls, and once he was up the tree he began eating all the ripe persimmons, and the only ones he threw down to the crab were green and hard. One of them hit the crab on the head and hurt him badly.

The crab was naturally angry and asked three of his friends, a mortar and a hornet and a chestnut, to help him punish the monkey. So these three friends hid themselves around the crab's house one day, and the crab invited the monkey to come to tea.

When the monkey arrived he was given a seat by the fire. The chestnut was hiding in the ashes, roasting itself, and suddenly it burst out of the fireplace and burned the monkey on the neck. The monkey screamed with pain and jumped up. At that instant the hornet flew down and stung the monkey. Then the monkey started to run out of the house, but the mortar was sitting up above the door and fell down with a thud on the monkey, almost breaking his back.

The monkey finally saw there was no escape. So he bowed down low to the crab and his three friends and said: "I really did a bad thing when I ate all Mr. Crab's good persimmons and threw the green, hard ones at him. I promise never to do such a bad thing again. Please forgive me."

The crab accepted the monkey's apology, and they all became good friends again. The monkey had learned his lesson and never again tried to cheat anyone.

The Crab and the Monkey

The Ogre and the Cock

THERE was a mountain so high and steep that it seemed to touch the sky. And on top of the mountain there lived an ogre. He was a terrible ogre with blue skin and a single horn growing out of the top of his head, and he was always doing wicked things.

One morning the farmers living near the mountain went out to work in their fields and found all their vegetables ruined. Somebody had pulled them up and trampled on them until there was not a single good one left. Who could have done such a thing? They looked very carefully and, sure enough, it was that wicked ogre. They could see prints of his big feet all over their fields.

This made the farmers very angry. They were tired of this ogre's tricks. They looked at all their ruined vegetables and became still angrier. Then they looked up at the mountain and all yelled at the same time: "O you wicked ogre! Why don't you quit doing these wicked things?"

The ogre looked down at them from the top of the mountain and answered in a terrible voice: "You must give me a human being each day for my supper. Then I'll quit bothering you."

The farmers had never heard of such an impudent ogre. They shook their tools at the ogre and roared: "Who do you think you are, wanting to eat a human being each day!"

"I'm the ogre-est ogre in all the land," the ogre roared back. "That's who I am! There's absolutely nothing I can't do! Ha! ha! ha!" The ogre's

voice echoed loudly through the mountains and made all the trees sway and toss.

"All right then," yelled the farmers. "Let's see if you're so wonderful. To prove it, in a single night you must build a stone stairway of one hundred steps from our fields all the way to the top of your mountain. If you can do that, then you can do anything and we'll just have to do whatever you want."

"I'll do it!" the ogre yelled back. "If I haven't finished the stairway before the first cock crows in the morning, then I promise to go away and never bother you again."

The Ogre and the Cock 99

As soon as it grew dark that night, the ogre crept into the farmyard and put a straw hood over the head of every single chicken so they couldn't see when the sun began to rise. Then he said: "Now I'll build that stairway." And he set to work very hard, building a stairway right up the mountain.

He worked so hard and so fast that he already had ninety-nine steps in place. Then the sun began to rise in the east. But he only smiled to himself, thinking that the cocks wouldn't crow at all and that he'd still have plenty of time to put the last stone in place.

But there was also a good fairy who lived on the mountain. The fairy had been watching and had seen what a mean trick the ogre was playing. So while the ogre was going down for the last stone, the fairy flew down and took a hood off the head of one of the cocks.

The cock saw the sun rising and crowed loudly: *"ko-ke-kok-ko!"* This woke up all the other cocks, who had thought it was still night because of the straw hoods over their heads, and they all began to crow.

The ogre was very surprised when he heard this. "I've lost!" he cried. "And there was just one more stone to go." But even ogres must keep their promises, so he stroked his horn very sadly and went away far into the mountains.

No one ever saw the ogre again and the farmers lived very happily beside the mountain. They finished the stairway up the mountain and often went up it on summer evenings to enjoy the view.

The Rabbit Who Crossed the Sea

ONCE there was a white rabbit who wanted to cross the sea. Across the waves he could see a beautiful island and he wanted very badly to go there. But he couldn't swim and there were no boats. Then he had an idea.

He called to a shark in the sea and said: "Oh, Mr. Shark, which one of us has the most friends, you or I?"

"I'm sure I have the most friends," said the shark.

"Well, let's count them to make sure," said the rabbit. "Why don't you have your friends line up in the sea between here and that island over there? Then I can count them."

So the sharks all lined up in the sea, and the rabbit went hopping from the back of one shark to the next, counting, "one, two, three, four . . . ." Finally he reached the island.

Then he turned to the sharks and said: "Ha, ha! You dumb sharks. I certainly fooled you. I got you to make a bridge for me, without your even knowing it."

The sharks became very angry. One of them reached up with his long snout and snatched off a piece of the rabbit's fur.

"Oh, it hurts!" cried the rabbit and began weeping.

Just then the king of the island came by. He asked the rabbit what was the matter, and when he'd heard the rabbit's story, he said: "You musn't ever fool others and tell lies again. If you promise to be good, I'll tell you how you can get your fur back."

"Oh, I promise, I promise," said the rabbit.

So then the king gathered some bulrushes and made a nest with them. "Now you sleep here in this nest of bulrushes all night," said the king, "and your fur will grow back."

The rabbit did as he was told. Next morning he went to the king and said: "Thank you very, very much. My fur all grew back and I'm well again. Thank you, thank you, thank you."

Then the rabbit went hopping off along the seashore, dancing and singing. He never tried to fool anyone again.

The Grateful Statues

ONCE upon a time an old man and an old woman were living in a country village in Japan. They were very poor and spent every day weaving big hats out of straw. Whenever they finished a number of hats, the old man would take them to the nearest town to sell them.

One day the old man said to the old woman: "New Year's is the day after tomorrow. How I wish we had some rice-cakes to eat on New

Year's Day! Even one or two little cakes would be enough. Without some rice-cakes we can't even celebrate New Year's."

"Well, then," said the old woman, "after you've sold these hats, why don't you buy some rice-cakes and bring them back with you?"

So early the next morning the old man took the five new hats that they had made, and went to town to sell them. But after he got to town he was unable to sell a single hat. And to make things still worse, it began to snow very hard.

The old man was very sad as he began trudging wearily back toward his village. He was going along a lonesome mountain trail when he suddenly came upon a row of six stone statues of Jizo, the protector of children, all covered with snow.

"My, my! Now isn't this a pity," the old man said. "These are only stone statues of Jizo, but even so just think how cold they must be standing here in the snow."

"I know what I'll do!" the old man suddenly said to himself. "This will be just the thing."

So he unfastened the five new hats from his back and began tying them, one by one, on the heads of the Jizo statues.

When he came to the last statue he suddenly realized that all the hats were gone. "Oh, my!" he said, "I don't have enough hats." But then he remembered his own hat. So he took it off his head and tied it on the head of the last Jizo. Then he went on his way home.

When he reached his house the old woman was waiting for him by the fire. She took one look at him and cried: "You must be frozen half to death. Quick! come to the fire. What did you do with your hat?"

The old man shook the snow out of his hair and came to the fire. He told the old woman how he had given all the new hats, and even his own

hat, to the six stone Jizo. He told her he was sorry that he hadn't been able to bring any rice-cakes.

"My! that was a very kind thing you did for the Jizo," said the old woman. She was very proud of the old man, and went on: "It's better to do a kind thing like that than to have all the rice-cakes in the world. We'll get along without any rice-cakes for New Year's."

By this time it was late at night, so the old man and woman went to bed. And just before dawn, while they were still asleep, a very wonderful thing happened. Suddenly there was the sound of voices in the distance, singing:

"A kind old man walking in the snow
Gave all his hats to the stone Jizo.
So we bring him gifts with a yo-heave-ho!"

The voices came nearer and nearer, and then you could hear the sound of footsteps on the snow.

The sounds came right up to the house where the old man and woman were sleeping. And then all at once there was a great noise, as though something had been put down just in front of the house.

The old couple jumped out of bed and ran to the front door. When they opened it, what do you suppose they found? Well, right there at the door someone had spread a straw mat, and arranged very neatly on the mat was one of the biggest and most beautiful and freshest rice-cakes the old people had ever seen.

"Whoever could have brought us such a wonderful gift?" they said, and looked about wonderingly.

They saw some tracks in the snow leading away from their house. The snow was all tinted with the colors of dawn, and there in the distance, walking over the snow, were the six stone Jizo, still wearing the hats which the old man had given them.

The old man said: "It was the stone Jizo who brought this wonderful rice-cake to us."

The old woman said: "You did them a kind favor when you gave them your hats, so they brought this rice-cake to show their gratitude.

The old couple had a very wonderful New Year's Day celebration after all, because now they had this wonderful rice-cake to eat.

The Bobtail Monkey

ONCE there was a monkey who was very young and foolish. He was always playing tricks and doing very foolish, dangerous things. All the other monkeys kept telling him he ought to be more careful or someday he'd get hurt, but he just wouldn't listen to them at all.

One day he was racing through the forest, climbing the highest trees and swinging from the longest vines, and he was so careless that, all of a sudden, he fell down out of the trees, right into the middle of a thorn bush. A long, sharp thorn went right through the tip of his tail.

"Ouch! Oh! Ouch!" he cried. "Oh, how it hurts!" And then he began bawling very loudly, for you see this foolish monkey wasn't a brave monkey at all.

Just then a barber came walking by, carrying his razor with him. When the monkey saw him, he said: "Please, Mr. Barber cut this thorn out of my tail."

So the barber got out his razor and started to cut the thorn out. But remember, this foolish monkey wasn't a brave monkey at all. So when he saw the razor getting near his tail, he yelled: "Oh, it's going to hurt!" And with those words he gave a big jump. The razor went right through his tail, cutting the tip of it right off!

When the monkey saw this, he became very angry. "Just look what you've done to my tail!" he said. "You must put my tail back on for me, or if you don't you'll have to give me your razor.

Of course the barber couldn't put the monkey's tail back on, so instead he gave the monkey his razor. Then the foolish monkey went walking away through the forest, carrying the razor with him. He looked very silly with a bobbed tail, but he was so proud of the razor that he didn't even think about his tail.

Presently the monkey saw an old woman who was gathering wood. Some of the wood was too long and she was trying to break it to make it short enough to carry home. The monkey watched her a little while. He wanted very much to show someone his beautiful razor, and this seemed like a good chance. So he said: "Look, Granny, I have a wonderful razor, which is very sharp. You may borrow it to cut your wood."

The old woman was very pleased. "Thank you very much, Mr. Monkey," she said, and began cutting the wood with the monkey's razor.

Now, a razor is not meant for cutting wood, and very soon the monkey's razor became all ragged, full of notches and scratches.

When the monkey saw this, he became very angry. "Just look what you've done to my razor!" he said. "You must give it back to me just the way it was before, or if you don't you'll have to give me all this firewood you've gathered."

Of course the old woman couldn't repair the razor, so instead she gave the monkey her firewood. Then the foolish monkey went walking away through the forest, carrying the firewood with him. He looked very silly with a bobbed tail, but he was so proud of the firewood that he didn't even think about his tail.

Presently the monkey saw another old woman who was baking cookies. Now, the monkey loved cookies better than anything and wanted some very badly. So he said: "Look, Granny, I have some wonderful firewood which is very dry. You may borrow it to bake your cookies."

The old woman was very pleased, because the wood she was using was green and wouldn't burn well. "Thank you very much, Mr. Monkey," she said. She took the monkey's firewood and put it on the fire.

Now, dry firewood burns very hot and fast, and the fire burned very brightly. The monkey stood watching until the cookies were all baked.

Oh, how good they smelled. He stood there licking his lips. Finally the old woman began to take the cookies off the fire. By this time the firewood was all burned to ashes.

When the monkey saw this, he became very angry. "Just look what you've done to my firewood!" he said. "You must give it back to me just the way it was before, or if you don't you'll have to give me all these cookies you've baked."

"But how can I give the firewood back?" asked the woman. "You saw it burn up in the fire."

"I can't help that," said the monkey. "You must give it back, or if you don't you'll have to give me the cookies."

Of course the old woman couldn't change the ashes back into firewood, so instead she gave the monkey all the cookies, piping hot from the oven, all stacked in a bowl. Then the foolish monkey went walking away through

the forest, carrying the bowl and nibbling on the delicious cookies. He looked very silly with a bobbed tail, but he was so busy eating cookies that he didn't even think about his tail.

Presently the monkey saw an old man who was carrying a beautiful gong made of brass. Now wouldn't it be wonderful, he told himself, to have a gong like that, so everyone would listen to me. There were still quite a few cookies left, so he said: "Look, Grandpop, I have some delicious cookies. I'll trade them for that old gong of yours." And he gave the old man one of the cookies to try.

The old man ate the cookie. It was so delicious that he very much wanted some more. "All right," he said, "you take the gong and I'll take the cookies."

Then the foolish monkey took the gong and climbed to the very top of the highest tree in the forest, way up where the branches were thin and bendy. He looked very silly with a bobbed tail, but he was so proud of himself and his brass gong that he didn't even think about his tail. He began beating the gong very hard and singing in a loud voice, so loud that all the monkeys in the forest could hear him. This is the song he sang:

I'm a handsome little monkey,
The smartest in the land;
With my fine brass gong,
I'm the leader of the band.
Bong! Bong! B-O-N-G!!!

I had a pretty tail,
Which I traded for a razor,
Which I traded for some wood,
Which I traded for some cookies,
Which I traded for a gong—
A fine brass gong.
Bong! BONG! B-O-N-G!!!

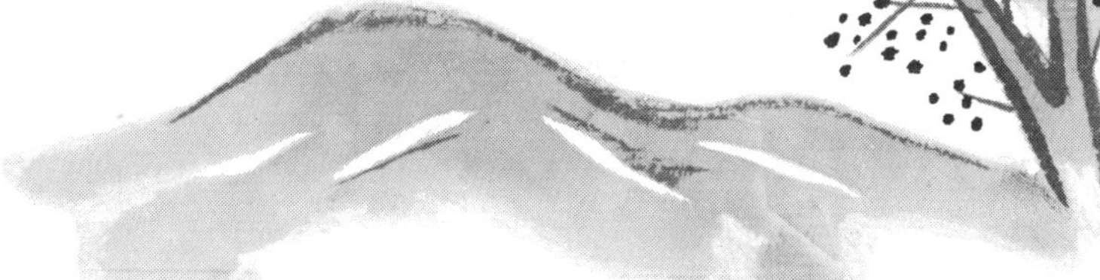

How the foolish monkey sang, looking very silly as he waved his bobbed tail in the air where all the other monkeys could see it. But on the last "Bong!" he hit the gong so hard that he fell right out of the tree, all the way to the ground, right into another thorn bush! How all the other monkeys laughed as they pulled the thorns out of him! After that they always called him Bobtail Bong-bong, and never again did he forget about his tail.